William Leman Rede

The Rake's Progress

A Drama in Three Acts

William Leman Rede

The Rake's Progress
A Drama in Three Acts

ISBN/EAN: 9783337376840

Printed in Europe, USA, Canada, Australia, Japan

Cover: Foto ©Andreas Hilbeck / pixelio.de

More available books at **www.hansebooks.com**

THE

RAKE'S PROGRESS

A DRAMA

IN

THREE ACTS.

BY

WILLIAM LEMAN REDE.

AUTHOR OF

The Loves of the Stars—His First Champagne—Faith and
Falsehood—Judgment of Paris—City Games—Barn
Burners—Douglas Travestie—Saloon and Cellar—
Boyhood of Bacchus, &c., &c.

THOMAS HAILES LACY,

89, STRAND,

(*Opposite Southampton Street, Covent Garden Market,*)

LONDON.

COSTUMES.

Tom Rakewell.—Scarlet hunting frock, buckskin breeches, top boots.—*2nd dress.*—Jockey jacket and cap.—*3rd dress.*—Modern ball room dress.—*4th dress.*—Surtout and white trousers.—*5th dress.*—Fleshings, tattered garments, and a blanket.

Harry Markham.—Riding dress.—*2nd dress.*—Jockey jacket, be-mudded.—*3rd dress.*—Ball room dress.—*4th dress.*—Walking dress.

Frederick Florid.—Modern suit.

Sam Slap.—Green coat, striped waistcoat, many under waistcoats, white cord breeches, top boots, white hat.—*2nd dress.*—Of the same description, but not so good.—*3rd dress.*—Apparently the same clothes but very old and shabby.

Ned Nokes.—Smart groom's livery.—*2nd dress.*—A different livery.—*3rd dress.*—A groom's undress, old, but not ragged.

Snump.—Corduroy breeches, white stockings, high lows, dark waistcoat, grey fustian coat, coloured neckerchief, and old brown hat.

Briggs.—Handsome, but flash modern suit.

Frank and Market People—Countrymen's frocks and coats.

Fanny Moreland.—Half mourning.—*2nd dress.*—Ball room dress.—*3rd dress.*—White muslin.

Lady Blazon.—Three dresses, in the extreme of fashion.

Betty.—Half mourning.—*2nd and 3rd dress.*—Dress of a lady's maid in humble life.

Peggy and Martha.—As lady's maids.

Market Women.—Country open gowns, straw hats.

TIME IN PERFORMANCE.—2 hours and 10 minutes.

THE RAKE'S PROGRESS.

ACT I.

SCENE I.—*A Market Place.* (*3rd grooves.*)

BETTY, *and* MALE *and* FEMALE PEASANTS, *with baskets containing eggs, ducks, &c., discovered.*

Enter FRANK, R.

FRANK. Well, Betty, busy marketing, eh?

BETTY. Busy! ay, that I am; I work like a galley slave! What with furbishing the house, attending to the dairy, and looking after my young missus, I've my hands full depend on't.

FRANK. Ah, poor Miss Fanny Moreland!

BETTY. Poor Miss Fanny! well, I'm sure! Why though her father died what they call an *insolent* debtor, poor Miss Fanny has two hundred pounds a-year under her mother's will, and a house to live in, and every comfort, and me for a waiting maid.

FRANK. Well, I meant no harm when I said poor Miss Fanny, for every one loves her.

BETTY. Ay, every human soul, down to the cat. She's had a iddication fit for a duchess; and poor Mr. Moreland (he was poor if you like) though once a great merchant, died without a penny. Yet, what o' that—riches never made a gentleman. But I can't stand talking to you, I'm so busy. He died and left my missus an orphan, and what o' that—she's independent.

FRANK. Well, but I've news for you.

BETTY. I can't stop to hear it—I am so busy. It's about Mary Briggs—why Jack Jenkins will no more marry she than you will.

FRANK. But it ain't of her, it is—

BETTY. I know—and I'd stop and hear it, if I wasn't so busy—it's about Widow Muggle and her children; well, if ever I did see such a woman as that. I went the other morning—

I'd tell you, if 1 warn't so busy—and I saw her washing three of her children in a tea-cup ; she is the most lazy, idle, loiter-g cretur—only I can't bear to speak ill of any one, or else I)uld tell you.

FRANK. Well, but I've some news—

BETTY. I can't stay to hear it, I'm so busy. (*going.*)

FRANK. Oh, but it concerns your missus.

BETTY. Eh? well I will hear that.

FRANK. Old Rakewell, the miser, is dead.

BETTY. Gone, is he? well I don't pity him—not a bit ; a nasty, creeping, cranky, dingy, stingy fellow ; he had more money and less charity than any one in our parish ; he would have skinned a flint, and made soup of the parings. Well, what's this to my missus?

FRANK. Why young Rakewell is his heir.

BETTY. Master Rakewell?

FRANK. Yes.

BETTY. Do tell me—though I am so busy I can hardly wait —what did that horrid old fellow die worth?

FRANK. Five thousand a-year, they do say, and a mort of money beside.

BETTY. And left it all to young squire?

FRANK. All—every penny.

BETTY. Well, he warn't such a bad fellow arter all—I always said as that old man had some good in him. Oh, this will be news to Miss Fanny ! I wish I warn't so busy, I'd hear more on't. Why Miss and Mr. Rakewell—squire, I mean—has been all the same as betrothed these twelve months. How happy she will be—and how happy shall I be ! Miss Fanny will ride in her own coach, as her father used, and I—I shall be my lady's lady. I wish I warn't so busy, Frank—but nothing's done if I ain't at home. I must go—poor dear old Mr. Rake-well, of Addle Street—

1*st* WOMAN. Eggs ! eggs !

BETTY. My missus and young squire will make a dear sweet pair.

2*nd* WOMAN. Ducks ! ducks !

BETTY. Oh, don't bother ! Dear, I wish I warn't so busy, I'd stop and have a rare gossip ! and yet, I must hurry home and tell my dear Miss Fanny. Oh, dear ! how happy she will be. Good bye, Frank—I would stop, but I'm so busy.

Exeunt FRANK, R., BETTY L.

SCENE II.—*A Chamber.* (*1st grooves.*)

HARRY MARKHAM. (*without*, L.) Lunch for one, horses for two, and brandy and water for ever so many.

Enters, with NED NOKES, L.

Well, Ned, we've smoked along famously to this old-fashioned village—built in the year one, I suppose. I'd sooner be buried in London than live here. How far are we from old Rakewell's domus ?

NOKES. About five miles and a half—or, correctly speaking, about fifteen minutes—that's the finish.

MARK. No, no, Ned—a mile in three minutes won't do for an inn hack. I wonder if Tom Rakewell is much changed. This windfall to him is a lucky hit—five thousand a-year, and about forty thousand in ready. My exchequer's below zero.

NOKES. Yes, sir, I must own that the mopusses have been shy of late. Never mind, sir, the book looks well for the Derby, and the St. Ledger's a safe card.

MARK. A thousand or two would see me through the next month, and then the devil may care ; one can but shoot or marry at last.

NOKES, Law, sir ! you wouldn't commit suicide ?

MARK. Why, rather than marry, I would ; just as I'd sooner kill a racehorse that put him in a mill.

FLORID. (*singing without*, L.)
"Diana, my beloved! I call in vain."

MARK. As I live and breathe that is Fred Florid ! Ned, holloa for one, but enough for two.

NOKES. (*calling.*) Mr. Florid !

FLORID. (*sings, without.*) "Echo hears, and calls again."

MARK. No—echo don't, but I do. Fred, my musical maniac —Fred !

FLORID. (*sings, without.*)
"Her mimic voice repeats the name around,
"And with Fred Florid all the walls resound."

Enter FLORID, L.

MARK. Fred Florid, my Memnon, how are you ? Why, what the devil brings you to this out-of-the-way village ?

FLORID. (*sings.*) "While the lads of the village," &c. The fact is, my dear Harry, I'm going on a visit to a sporting friend —this village lay in my way, and I wished to be out of the way of—

MARK. (c.) John Doe and Richard Roe, eh ?

FLORID. Yes, they haunt me still. But you, Harry—you—

MARK. I am down to visit a young fellow who has fallen into an immense fortune, and wants a judicious friend to help him to dispense it.

FLORID. His name?

MARK. Tom Rakewell.

FLORID. Indeed! I know the youth.

MARK. Ah! how came you to know him?

FLORID. (*sings*.) " We met—'twas in a crowd—
    And I thought he would shun me."

MARK. Don't sing, but talk, man alive. I mean to show young Rakewell something of the world—to bring him out.

NOKES. (R.—*aside*.) Or take him in—that's the finish

MARK. What say you—will you come down to this old ramshackle house, where the old miser, Rakewell, died? between us, we will show the heir a thing or two. Ned! dinner for two, horses for three, and the bill to follow.

NOKES. Yes, sir; be ready in a crack—that's the finish.

Crosses and exit L.

MARK. Well, Fred—does fortune still frown?

FLORID. Yes.

MARK. What, no luck at *rouge et noir?* no success on the turf? Well, I confess I'm confoundedly down myself—regularly cleaned out.

FLORID. So am I—I want a friend.

MARK. Then why the devil don't you go and take one? here's young Rakewell—if we don't have him, somebody else will. He is rolling in riches, and we may as well have it as others.

FLORID. Very true, Harry—but I'm in love.

MARK. In what? in love! I've been in debt, in danger, in gaol, and in jeopardy, but I was never in love in my life. Who and what is she? where did you meet her.

FLORID. (*sings*.) " I met her at the Fancy Fair."

MARK. D——n it, don't sing! Wherever woman smiles, pleasure beckons—wherever I go, I ask jollity for one. As to love, it's very well upon paper, but it won't do in fact. We fellows who roll through life, have nothing to do with it. Happiness is a household; while pleasure is a roamer who wanders to all places, and is everywhere to be met. Are you serious?

FLORID. Yes—I am in love with Diana Dulcet. A sweet girl, dark eyes, raven hair, and such an ancle!

MARK. I should have thought more of the description, if you had said—such money in the funds, such landed property, and such expectations.

FLORID. Ah, but she has them too.

MARK. That alters the case—get a parson for two as soon as

possible. If I could meet a woman with every charm, and half a million of money, I'd do the desperate myself. But come, luncheon waits, and our horses are ready ; a chop for two, and a gallop to follow.

FLORID. (*sings.*) " Mark, march, Ettrick and Teviotdale !"

Exeunt L.

SCENE III.—*An Old-fashioned Chamber.   Table, three chairs, deed-box, rouleaus, parchments, pens, ink, and paper.* (4*th grooves.*)

TOM RAKEWELL *and* TAILOR, *measuring him,* L. LAWYER *writing at table,* R.

LAWYER. The gross amount of cash in the house is seven thousand six hundred and forty pounds, sir ; securities for thirty-two thousand pounds outstanding, and the annual rental is—

RAKE. Why, I shall never spend half what you have named. Forty thousand pounds to one like myself, who never anticipated more than a couple of hundreds per annum ! Poor uncle Rakewell ! he was an unkind brother, but he has made amends for his harshness to my father, by kindness to his son.

LAWYER. Your uncle was a great man—a very great man. He left besides, five thousand a year.   He held more mortgages than any man within five counties.

TAILOR. I suppose you'll have your things of the newest fashion.

RAKE. Yes, yes.

HARRY MARKHAM. (*without,* L.) Stand for no repairs, young man—room for one.

Enter HARRY MARKHAM, L.

MARK. Ah, Tom ! my prince of Plutus, give me your hand ! Why, have you forgotten an old crony ?

RAKE. Forgotten—oh, no ; but I haven't seen you since you quitted the country for a town life.

MARK. True—a life of pleasure made me forget even you; but I heard of your fortune, and came instantly to congratulate you.   So, Tom, the old hunks has popped off at last, and left his ill-gotten gold.   I wish every noble-minded fellow like you had such a rich old rascal for an uncle.

RAKE. Hush, hush ! remember that rich old rascal has made me what I am.   Don't let us say any ill of him now he's in his grave.

MARK. Right, praise the bridge that carries you safely over.

To be sure, he couldn't carry his gold away with him, or he would. Who's that guy?

(looking at the TAILOR, *who comes down* R.

RAKE. My tailor.

MARK. That a tailor! Spectacles for one! I never saw such a fellow. Where are you from? *(crosses to* C.)

TAILOR. From London, sir.

MARK. From London!—yes, and a confounded long way from London, I guess. Tom—my dear Tom, I am your friend; this will never do. I must take you to Stultz. I wouldn't wear a coat of such a fellow's making—no, not to be hanged in !

RAKE. But, my dear Harry, this person has worked for my father all his life.

MARK. Psha! what of that? He looks old enough to have breeched Noah. I say, whereabouts did you live at the time of the fire of London? There, don't gape, but be off; take your departure for one.

TAILOR. Sir—

MARK. Be off, I say !   *Exit* TAILOR, R.

My dear Tom, I'll arrange this matter for you. You must go to Stultz—everybody does it.

RAKE. Oh, if everybody does it, then indeed—

MARK. Yes, yes—leave it all to me. Who's he?

RAKE. That's my lawyer.

MARK. Lawyer! My dear Tom, you mustn't keep such bad company. A lawyer's very well when one wants money, but never otherwise. I say, Mr. Thingamy.

RAKE. His name's not Mr. Thingamy.

MARK. No matter—Mr. Rakewell's engaged.

LAWYER. I only wished—

RAKE. You can finish the inventory at your leisure.

LAWYER. Oh, very well, sir—I would not intrude—*(rises.)*

MARK. Oh, but you do intrude; there, toddle, and take your blue bag along with you,   *Exit* LAWYER, R.

Well, Tom, your hand. Life lies before you—a world of pleasure without a taint of care. A young handsome dog—don't blush, no one does it—you must dash on—you must be one of us. What do you propose?—you'll not stay in this dull village ?

RAKE. My father lived and died in it.

MARK. Ah, it may do to die in, but hang me if one can live in it. No, no, you must come to London.

RAKE. Why, I—

MARK. You must—everybody does it,

RAKE. Oh, then, indeed—

MARK. I'll tell you what Tom, I have a sincere friendship for you, and though I haven't seen you these five years, I have often talked about you—I'll introduce you to some fellows after your own heart—men of spirit and fashion. You must join our clubs.

RAKE. Why, my life has been so secluded, that—

MARK. Pshaw! everybody does it. You'll subscribe to Tattersall's, of course—everybody does it ; mingle at Almack's —trifle on the turf—in fact, you must and shall be a highly finished fellow. You're born for the world, and must bustle in it—everybody does it. By-the-bye, I've brought an old friend of yours with me—Fred Florid.

RAKE. Fred Florid—Florid—you mistake ; he's no friend of mine—I don't know him.

MARK. Oh, yes, yes, you do—everybody knows him.

RAKE. Oh, then, I know him, of course.

MARK. Ned!

Enter NED NOKES, L.

NOKES. Sir.

MARK. Shew Mr. Florid up ; and see if any of the servants can let you have champagne for three, and devilled biscuits to follow—hey?

RAKE. Certainly. But young man—Harry, I am afraid we have no champagne in the house ; but we have capital Madeira, and if you'll see Mrs. Hartshorn, the old house-keeper—

MARK. A housekeeper?—do you keep a housekeeper? I would as soon think of keeping a lady's maid! You must have a valet ; pray consider my fellow as yours. Ned, wait on Mr. Rakewell.

NOKES. I will, sir. I'm hired—that's the finish. *Exit* L.

MARK. Ned will just suit—don't say a word, he's your man. He's the very fellow for you—knows the world and has seen life ; and so must you—everybody does it.

FLORID. (*without, singing.*) "Do you remember the first time I met you."

RAKE. Curse me if I do, for I never saw you before.

Enter FLORID, L.

FLORID. Well, Tom, how goes it? Do you remember our jolly party, five years ago, at Squire Briarley's, when you were so full of wit and humour—all dance and jollity?

RAKE. Oh, yes, yes, I remember—(*aside.*) nothing at all about it.

MARK. Come, come, my boy, you've not forgotten Fred. Sit down, sit down, make yourself at home. (*goes to* R. *table.*)

Enter NOKES, L., *with wine.*

FLORID. (*sings.*) " A bumper of Burgundy fill, fill for me,
Give those who prefer it, champagne."

MARK. Tom, my boy, here's "health to enjoy your fortune !"
Fred, here's " may you get rid of that singing in your head!"
Come, Tom, a toast.

RAKE. (*sitting at back of table.*) I really scarcely know—

MARK. Don't be shy—courage for one. Is there no little
blue-eyed, cherry-cheeked, lovely-lipped Hebe in this corner of
the globe? What, another blush! There he is, Fred, drawn
from life, and coloured after nature. Come, her name ?

RAKE. Why, if I must—

MARK. Everybody does it.

RAKE. Well, then, here's " Fanny !"

MARK. Bumpers for three.

FLORID. (*sings.*) " Of all the girls that are so smart,
There's none like blue-eyed Fanny,
She is the darling of your heart,
And she lives in yonder valley."

RAKE. Why, how do you know she lives in yonder valley ?

MARK. Oh, everybody knows it. Here's " Fanny !" (*they
rise and drink.*) Fanny's a very pretty name, and I dare say
Fanny's a very pretty girl ; but you will soon be in the metro-
polis, the court of beauty, and the bower of love. This seems
a very dull place. What shall we do? Come, a frolic for
three—what's stirring, Ned ?

NED. (L.) Nothing, sir, all's as dead as small beer. I've been
all about, and couldn't raise a row no how.

MARK. Shall we have a touch at hazard?

RAKE. I never play.

MARK. Never play ?—everybody does it.

NOKES. There isn't a pair of dice in the place.

FLORID. No dice !

MARK. No dice ! What an infernal slow neighbourhood !

NOKES. What do you say, sir, to a steeple chase ?

MARK. Capital ! Horses for three. Tom, I know you are a
famous rider, and Fred's a perfect phæton—arn't you Fred ?

FLORID. Yes, but my horse is such a sorry hack.

MARK. Hack, be hanged ! you must have a hunter. Ned !

NOKES. Sir !

MARK. Wasn't Sam Slap, the horse dealer, at the last town
when we left it ?

NOKES. Yes, sir—and training some of the prettiest creatures
you ever saw.

MARK. Ned, put yourself outside my mare; send Sam to me with the best of his stud, and jockey jackets and caps for three—vanish! (*rises.*)

NOKES. I will, sir. A steeple chase! break all their necks—that's the finish. *Exit, L.*

MARK. (L.) You must do something—notoriety's the thing—make a bold dash—fame for one. We'll have a race for a cool two hundred—come, I'll book it. Oh, you need not dub the cash—nobody does it; to-morrow's settling day.

FLORID. (C.) And to-morrow must be racing-day, I think. It will be some hours ere Ned returns.

MARK. No such thing—Ned's gone off like a rocket! Sam will be here like a flash of lightning.

RAKE. (R.) I must leave you for awhile, Harry—I have an appointment.

MARK. Hey! what, the petticoat fever? Well, I'll give you an hour.

RAKE. One hour! oh, more than—

MARK. No—I'll time you. Women are the prettiest play-things in the world, but we mustn't let them interfere with the serious business of life. Nobody stays more than an hour with their lady love.

RAKE. Nobody? well then, I won't.

MARK. That's right. You'll be back by four, start by five, know the winner by six, return to dinner by seven, and then off for London, my boy!

Exeunt, RAKEWELL, R., MARKHAM *and* FLORID, L.

SCENE IV.—*A Chamber.* (*2nd grooves.*)

Enter FANNY, R. 2 E., *with a letter.*

FANNY. I wonder Rakewell is not here; he did not use to overstay his time;—oh! but at this moment a thousand things are calling his attention; the sudden news of his fortune—the affairs of his deceased uncle, must distract him. Kind, kind Rakewell—your first thought on hearing of your own happiness, was to secure mine. (*reads.*) " Possessed of a large fortune—you only are wanting to make me the most blessed of beings."

Enter BETTY, L.

BETTY. Oh, miss! I am in such a bustle; here's a coach coming along smack up to this house.

FANNY. Well, is that so strange?

BETTY. Why, I'm sure I an't seen one here—no—not since—

FANNY. Betty!

BETTY. Lawk, miss, I beg pardon, I meant no harm ; only for the last year or two all the coaches seem to turn down t'other road ; now don't fret, Miss Fanny, I didn't say it to grieve you.

FANNY. The loss of carriage visitors would never grieve me ; there were other thoughts connected with your words.

BETTY. Never mind, Miss Fanny ; you mark my words, now young squire's rich, you'll ride in your own coach that is, his— which is all one. (*loud knock*, L.) Well, if that don't surprise our knocker, I shall wonder. Oh, gemini! what a smart looking footman—I'm in such a bustle. (*knock.*) Well, I'm coming—I'm in such a bustle.   *Exit* L.

FANNY. Who can this be ? not Rakewell, sure ; and other visitors, since my father's death, I as little expected as desired.

Enter BETTY *and* LADY BLAZON, L.

LADY B. Dear, dear Miss Moreland ; how do you do? you look lovely, but that you always did ; well, now, you'll think it unkind that I haven't been to see you.

FANNY. 'Tis two years, I think, since I had that pleasure.

LADY B. Yes, dear—heard of your sad affliction ; could not come, then.

BETTY. (*aside.*) Hang the friend, I say, that won't come in affliction. Ay! she's like all the rest of them.   *Exit* L.

LADY B. Nerves, nerves, dear ; I'm such a sensitive creature—feel everybody's grief as my own—all sympathy—I should have distressed you and destroyed myself.

FANNY. I hope you had pleasanter employment than comforting affliction ; you have been in London?

LADY B. Yes, dear, and I should have written to you, but what with parties by night, and gay scenes by day, I really couldn't snatch a moment ; and then I couldn't write without allusions that would have shocked my nerves.

FANNY. Pray make no further apology.

LADY B. I suppose you know I'm a widow? .

FANNY. Indeed!

LADY B. Yes—I buried my Goth twelve months ago ; you were always a prodigious favourite of his, in your father's lifetime.

FANNY. In my father's time, I believe I was.

LADY B. You must come and pass a few days at my seat, and then, dear, you must take a little trip to London—you must, indeed! moping in the country—it's quite horrid.

FANNY. I thank you, but I have now moped here for two years ; I bore this scene through the bitterest of my affliction, and it has become endeared to me.—What should I do in London?

LADY B. Do? what every body does, dear; dress, dance, sing, play, go to the opera, and flirt with the fellows.

Enter BETTY, L.

Betty. Oh, gemini! gemini! I'm in such a bustle;—here's young squire coming smoking along! old Dobbin gallops for dear life; I do believe that horse is as sensible as I am, and knows that his master is coming to you.

LADY B. Young Squire! do you mean Mr. Rakewell?

BETTY. I mean my missus' husband that is to be; young Squire Rakewell.

FANNY. For shame, Betty; you know I forbid this conversation.

BETTY. La, miss! where's the harm?—no shame in being married; I know it wouldn't make me ashamed a bit, and Squire Rakewell is the handsomest, nicest, goodnaturedest, and now the richest—

Enter RAKEWELL, L., *singing.*

RAKE. (*crossing to* FANNY, R.) Dear, dear Fanny!

LADY B. (L.) Not so bad—not so bad; but a Goth in manner.

FANNY. (*crosses* C.) Mr. Rakewell—Lady Blazon.

RAKE. I beg your pardon, Lady Blazon, but hurrying to my dear Fanny, I did not perceive you were present.

LADY B. (*aside.*) Quite a brute! Oh, don't name it, my dear sir—happy to congratulate and condole, and all that—have come to rob you of Miss Fanny for a few days; I can't prevail on her to go to my seat—you will be a more eloquent pleader. I'll leave you, Fanny dear, I shall see you again to-day, for you know I can't bear to be away from you.

(*shaking hands.*

BETTY. (L., *aside.*) Only two years at a time.

LADY B. (L. C.) Not a step; I'll find my way.

BETTY. Oh! I'll show you out, ma'am, and with the greatest of pleasure.

LADY B. Adieu! you *must* come, dear—Mr. Rakewell, good morning.   *Exit with* BETTY, L.

RAKE. (C.) Fanny, my darling Fanny, happiness is now in store for us; the instant the news came to me, you were my first thought— your house, my first visit.

FANNY. (R.) What detained you so long?

RAKE. An old friend, Harry Markham—a delightful companion, and so kind to me, that I couldn't get away—by-the-bye, I've promised to take a trip to town, to-day.

FANNY. To London?

RAKE. Yes, everybody does it; besides, he has promised to make me a suscriber to Tattersall's, and a member of his club.

FANNY. But why should you do this?

RAKE. I don't know why—but everybody does it.

FANNY. Ah! I fear these gay companions will lead your mind away from the calm enjoyment of domestic life.

RAKE. No, Fanny; a bit of a breeze now and then makes a calm more delightful; one must do as other people do—you really must go to Lady Blazon's—everybody goes there.

FANNY. No, no; I have no pleasure in such scenes.

RAKE. Well, that's the case with me; I've no pleasure in 'em, nor anyone else I believe; but then, everybody does it; n scene can have charms for me where you are not, and when forget you, Fanny, may I be myself forgotten; I picture to myself scenes of such rational, pure delight, unruffled by a cloud, serene as your smile, guileless and calm;—talking of calms, I'm going to ride a steeple-chase, to-day.

FANNY. A steeple-chase! my dear Rakewell.

RAKE. Why, everybody does it; and my friend Markham has brought with him one of the oldest friends I ever had, whom I never saw in my life before—one Fred Florid; and Harry, I, and he, are to gallop from my uncle's house to the steeple of Bransdon Church.

FANNY. Where he lies buried.

RAKE. I never thought of that; it's very wrong, to be sure, but everybody does it.

FANNY. Ah, Rakewell! Rakewell! the hand that reared churches, meant not their steeples for the racer's land-mark.

RAKE. That's very true—but everybody does it. Come, come, this is my first frolic, and shall be my last. Now, Fanny, you'll go and see us come in, won't you? Yes, I know you will, for I must see you before I start for London; come, won't you?

FANNY. It's very wrong—

RAKE. I know it's wrong—it's very wrong; but come, now, promise.

FANNY. Well, I do promise.

RAKE. Thanks, my dear Fanny—adieu! *Exit*, L.

FANNY. I dread these sudden friends, who come like swallows, when the summer shines, and leave us in the winter of distress. Betty!

Enter BETTY, L.

BETTY. Yes, miss.

FANNY. We are going to Bransdon Church.

BETTY. To church, miss?—what already?

FANNY. At least, near there. Mr Rakewell rides a race to-day; I have promised to be present at it; get your cloak and bonnet. *Exit* FANNY, R.

BETTY. I will, miss—oh! I'm in such a bustle. A race!—gemini! I hope he may win—t'others may break their necks, if they please, so that young squire wins—oh, I'm in such a bustle! *Exit*, L.

SCENE V.—*The Race Ground—Church in view*, R.

Enter SAM SLAP, *and* NED NOKES, L. 2 E.

SAM. Sold three horses in two minutes—vot a hidea! Ned, your master's a good one. Well, how are you, my pigeon?—why, when I see you last, you was waiter at the " Horns," in Yorkshire.

NOKES. Yes, but I left suddenly.

SAM. Something wrong, eh?—any of the maids pretty?—vot a killing hidea!

NOKES. No; something else.

SAM. Oh! I see—a little bit of the wrong, hey?—something missing?

NOKES. I'll tell you; missus didn't exactly know where she had put some of the plate.

SAM. But you did?—vot a hodd idea!

NOKES. And so there were some words, and I felt that it reflected on my character, and left—that's the finish.

SAM. Bolted, eh?—vot a natural hidea!

NOKES. No, not bolted, but I went off in the middle of the night.

SAM. Vot a dark hidea!

NOKES. Yes, rather than have any words—that's the finish. Well, what are you up to? I arn't seen you since you were a riding boy at Doncaster.

SAM. A riding boy! I was—look at me now; here's a figure for a riding boy—what a horse-back-breaking hidea! I got too fat for my trade, no horse could conweniently carry my weight; so instead of riding horses, I took to selling them. I say, Ned, there's your swag, (*giving money.*) and thank you for the customer. Three horses in two minutes!—vot a expeditious hidea!

NOKES. I say, I hope they're good ones ; if not, master deals no more—that's the finish !

SAM. Vy, vot do you expect in the time ?—but two of them are fairish—Blackball is by Furbelow, out of Diana—Spanker by Dash, out of Aurora.

NOKES. And t'other ?

SAM. He's a roarer, too !—vot a vindy hidea !—he's by old Bobby's cart horse, out of the miller's mare ; vot a pedigree !

NOKES. It's all right ; young Squire rides the blood ; my master, Blackball ; and Mr. Florid, the screw—if he gets a floorer it don't matter. *(faint cry, R. 2 E.)* Here they come, I hear the holloa—that's the finish !

SAM. I wonder whereabouts the roarer is, that hanimal vot goes about five miles an hour, and thinks he's galloping—vot a progressive hidea.

(shouts without, R., increasing in loudness till RAKEWELL enters.

NOKES. Come, come along—a sharp turn round the corner, and we shall see them come in. Run, run.   *Exit, R. U. E.*

SAM. Run, run !—I'm a nice figure for running—vot a preposterous hidea !   *Exit, R. U. E.·*

Enter LADY BLAZON, FANNY, and BETTY, L.

PEOPLE. *(shout without.)* Huzza ! huzza !

Enter FRANK, R. U. E.

FRANK. He's done it—he's won it ! hurrah ! hurrah !

LADY B. Who—who ?

FRANK. Young Squire, to be sure ! here he comes—here he comes !—hurrah ! hurrah !

Enter RAKEWELL, in a jockey's dress, R. U. E.

RAKE. Ah, my dear Fanny, here I am !

FANNY. Not hurt, I hope ?

RAKE. Not a whit—never better ; oh, it was a glorious race ! I wonder where Mr. Florid can have got to ?

FANNY. Did he not start with you ?

RAKE. Yes, he did start with us, and that was all. You see, we went off in a gentle canter, Harry and I, side by side, and Fred in the rear. Shortly after, Harry and I broke out into a light gallop, and we never saw Mr. Florid after that.

FANNY. No accident, I hope ?

RAKE. Only a gentle tumble, at the worst.

LADY B. But how did the race proceed, Mr. Rakewell ?

RAKE. Oh, famously !—Harry and I, after riding along very comfortably for some time, side by side, at last came to rather a high hedge, and a tolerably broad ditch. " Is it deep ? " said he—" never was in it," said I.—" St ! St !" said he, and over we went, clean as a whistle; dashed down the meadows, right over the furrows—up this field, and down that; at last, Harry said, "We'll neck and neck it home; at present, we'll part company." —"With all my heart," said I—"Good bye," said he—"Good luck," said I; and off we set, he one way—I the other. We rode down two parellel fields with hedge on each side—I could just see his horse's ears peeping above the hedge, and he could see my mare's performing the same operation on the opposite side of the way. When we came within five hundred yards of home (his animal, I could see, was at its best), dash at one moment, we came over the hedge together, into the high road; there we were, head, heel, and hand, as hard as we could go— you might have covered us with your handkerchief. I let out, threw the mud and slush from my horse's heels, into his horse's eyes—and won by six lengths. Hurrah! Oh, there's nothing like racing! (*retires up with* FANNY, L.)

BETTY. I knew he'd win—I saw it—bless him! he looks as if he was born for a jacket.   (*laugh outside*, R.

Enter MARKHAM *covered with mud*—SAM *and* NOKES, R. U. E.

SAM. I say, do you know you're conweying away mud without leave of the commissioners.

MARK. Yes, and a pretty considerable lot I carried away. Ned, fresh togs for one, and brandy and water to follow.
                                        Exit NOKES, L. U. E.

RAKE. How the devil came you in such a pickle?

MARK. Come, I like that! why, when you made your grand push for home, your mare slapped her hoofs into a slough, and sent a cloud of mud over me—enough for six!

RAKE. Where did you leave Florid?

MARK. I left him in a ditch.   (*horn sounds*, L.

Enter NOKES, L. U. E.

NOKES. Mr. Florid's come in, sir.

MARK. How did he come?

NOKES. He came by the mail—it was passing by—his horse pitched him down—the coach took him up—that's the finish!

SAM. (R.) Riding a steeple chase, and coming home by the mail; vot a sporting hidea!

MARK. Ned, take places for five—three ins and two outs.

NOKES. Suppose they haven't room, sir.

MARK. Turn the insides out.

NOKES. I will, sir—that's the finish.   *Exit* L. U. E.

MARK. Sam, you'll go with us.

SAM. To be sure I will—a pigeon to be plucked, and I not there—vot a foolish hidea! But I say, sir, you see how the land lies ; (*pointing to* RAKEWELL *and* FANNY.) touched at the heart—affected in'ards.

MARK. Yes ; that's it, Sam.

SAM. I guessed with half a hie ;—look'ee there—light brown mane—sweet pretty fetlocks—curved neck—small head—oh, that's the female.   (*horn heard.*

MARK. Yes ; and that's the mail.

SAM. Vot a coinciding hidea! Well, ladies, ta-ta!
                                                                    (*crossing to* L.

MARK. I'd advise you to take places for two!
                                                                    (*crossing to* L.

SAM. 'Cause I'm a fat one—I'll have two insides ;—vot a enormous hidea !   *Exit* L.

RAKE. Well, adieu, my love ! (*kisses* FANNY.)

MARK. Kisses for one—can't you make it for two?

RAKE. Be quiet, you dog—be quiet. Adieu, my dear Fanny, adieu !

Exeunt RAKEWELL *and* MARKWELL, L. U. E.—LADIES *remain and the coach is seen to pass from* L. *to* R. *at back, the lower part hidden by the hedge,* RAKEWELL, MARKWELL, FLORID, NOKES, COACHMAN, *and* GUARD, *seen on it.*

END OF ACT I.

ACT II.

SCENE I.—*A Chamber in Mrs. Dabbleditch's House.*
(*2nd grooves.*)

Enter MRS. DABBLEDITCH *and* PEGGY, R.

MRS D. Peggy.

PEGGY. Ma'am.

MRS. D. Has last night's revelling injured my looks?

PEGGY. No, indeed, ma'am. (*aside.*) I should wonder if it had.

MRS. D. 'Twas a delightful party. Young Rakewell is a pretty fellow, but a dolt, and as insensible to the charms of a fine woman as a statue.

PEGGY. La, ma'am, do you think so? I hear he's a very devil among the girls.

MRS. D. Girls, girls! what do you talk to me of girls for? you know I hate to hear the pale, paltry chits spoken of—it's quite indelicate.

PEGGY. La, ma'am!

MRS. D. Be silent! don't answer me? What's the hour? what's the hour, I say—why don't you speak?

PEGGY. Why, you told me to be silent, and not answer you.

MRS. D. Peggy, you're getting impertinent—and if there's one thing I hate more than another, it's conceit and impudence.

PEGGY. (aside.) That's odd, for you have plenty of both.

MRS. D. What is the hour?

PEGGY. Nearly one, ma'am.

MRS. D. Then I may soon expect Mr. Florid.

PEGGY, Mr. Florid, ma'am!

MRS. D. Yes, child, a dashing young fellow, whom I met at Lady Flashton's soirées. I lost a trifle to him at écarté; I gave him one of my glances, and I think it created a sensation.

PEGGY. No doubt, ma'am; but I thought Mr. Rakewell was your favourite?

MRS. D. So he was, but he is so bashful; he has been in London now six months, but his friend, Mr. Markham, has not inocculated him with his impudence.

PEGGY. Mr. Markham, ma'am, was once a little favourite of yours.

MRS. D. Why, Peggy, you know my good heart; I would snatch any young man from destruction—but he is a sad fellow, he cannot appreciate so rich a gift as a woman's tender heart; he's a libertine.

PEGGY. La, ma'am, did *you* find that out?

MRS. D. What do you mean, slut—it's quite indelicate. No man in his senses would offer me an insult.

PEGGY. No man with his eyesight would, I'll be bound.

(knock L.

MRS. D. 'Tis Mr. Florid. **Am I as I should be, Peggy?**

PEGGY. Oh, yes, ma'am.

FLORID. (*without* L., *singing.*) "Come shining forth, my dearest, with looks of warm delight."

MRS. D. 'Tis he! What a charming voice he has—it's an alarm to love! Peggy, leave us.

PEGGY. What, ma'am, will you receive him alone?

MRS. D. Yes, chit—my honour protects me anywhere.

PEGGY. (*aside.*) Your age will, anyhow.

Enter FLORID, L.

FLORID. (*singing.*) " Good morning to your nightcap."

(to PEGGY, who exits L.

Ah, good morning, dear madam. (*they sit.*) You see I am true to my appointment—I should say yours. But, pray, don't take me for a merciless creditor.

MRS. D. Oh, Mr. Florid, I shouldn't think you merciless at all; I judge by myself, for Heaven knows *I* am not. A hundred, I think, Mr. Florid—may I trouble you? (*gives note.*)

FLORID. No trouble at all. (*sings.*) "Your money is your friend, is it not," &c. Really a very sensible old woman. Dear madam, I am perhaps intruding, and—(*rises.*)

MRS. D. Why, you are not going, Mr. Florid? I want to speak to you.

FLORID. To speak to me! (*sings.*) "Bid me discourse, I will enchant," &c.

MRS. D. I take the liberty of a friend, dear Mr. Florid; I fear you're leading a life of excesses. I know these things—

FLORID. What excesses, ma'am?

MRS. D. Mr. Dabbleditch, who I married when I was fifteen, was a sad man.

FLORID. (*aside.*) So I should expect.

MRS. D. He was always flaunting at parties, and neglecting the sweets of home.

FLORID. (*sings.*) "Home, home, sweet, sweet home," &c.

MRS. D. Are these your sentiments? So are they mine— what a coincidence in feeling!

FLORID. (*sings.*) "Ah, there's nothing half so sweet in life as love's young dream."

MRS. D. I differ with *that* sentiment; I have known second love truer and happier than the first.

FLORID. To be sure, ma'am, practice makes perfect. For my part, I think a third or fourth, or—

MRS. D. Ah, I fear you are a gay deceiver. Really it is not discreet for me to remain with you.

FLORID. Hollo! this won't do! (*sings sarcastically.*) "Had I a heart for falsehood framed, I *ne'er* could injure *you.*"

MRS. D. Fascinating fellow!—do you indeed think so?

FLORID. I can't stand this. (*sings.*) "Oh, yes, believe me— oh, yes," &c.

MRS. D. I do believe—I will not distrust you; no, your passion is not feigned.

FLORID. My passion!—where did you hear of it?

MRS. D. I saw it in your glances.

FLORID. What then, madam, you have observed my little attentions to—

MRS. D. Don't, don't!—how can you?

FLORID. How can I!—what?

MRS. D. At so short an acquaintance to make a declaration.

FLORID. Why, madam, our souls were congenial. (*sings.*)

" Ah, sure a pair were never seen,
So justly formed to meet by nature."

MRS. D. You're a sad flatterer, but I will not be obdurate; in one word, I will be yours.

FLORID. You, madam!

MRS. D. Why do you stare so? Joy and ecstasy take away his breath. Come, come, I know how to encourage the timid bashfulness of youth; you have triumphed—I am yours.

FLORID. I say, ma'am, I beg your pardon, but there's some mistake; I was declaring a passion for Miss Diana Dulcet.

MRS. D. Miss Dulcet?

FLORID. Yes, the lady to whom you observed my "little attentions."

MRS. D. Why, did you not just now declare your passion for me?

FLORID. For you? (*sings.*) "Oh, no, I never mentioned it— I never said a word."

MRS. D. Oh! very well, sir—insult my feelings—trample on my budding affection.

FLORID. Budding?—blown by Jupiter!

MRS. D. Leave me, sir—leave me, if you can.

FLORID. Oh, yes, I can. Good morning, ma'am. 'Gad I wish I was safe out of the house.

MRS. D. Will you then leave me?

FLORID. (*sings.*) "March away, march away! march, march away!"   *Exit* L.

MRS. D. What! gone in earnest! Ah, the young men now-a-days are brutes; it's quite indelicate, I declare. They are such young puppies, they won't open their eyes to their own good. Miss Diana Dulcet—lath and plaster—aged eighteen. As Hamlet says, "Look on this picture and on that." I think the world's made up of boys and girls now-a-days. I'm sure, such children marrying, it's quite indelicate.   *Exit,* R.

SCENE II.—*A Street.* (*1st grooves.*)

Enter NED NOKES, R., *with letters.*

NOKES. Let me see, this is an answer to Lord L——'s invitation; that'll do presently. Call at Lady B——'s, and two more letters, and that's the finish. (SAM SLAP *sings without,* L.) Why, if that arn't Slippery Sam, the swell horse-dealer. Why, Sam! Sam!

Enter SAM SLAP, L.

SAM. Who'd a thought of meeting you, and walking promiscuous about the streets, too. What a cool hidea.

NOKES. Why, where have you been hiding yourself these three months, hey?

SAM. I arn't been hiding myself—one of my grooms struck for wages.

NOKES. Struck for wages?

SAM. Yes, knocked me down. Vot a pugilistic hidea! I was rather haggravated and I hit him with a stable whip, and did not observe, in my hurry, that I used the butt end.

NOKES. Was that the finish?

SAM. No, it wasn't. You know, Ned, there's little secrets in all trades—nothing particular wrong, but a little—

NOKES. About the edges.

SAM. Just so. Well, this here haggravating vagabond goes and peaches something about a horse as I sold that warn't exactly all as it might ha' been.

NOKES. I see ; another roarer.

SAM. Worser! this here hanimal was sich a impostor as I never seed in my life—he'd a made a capital war horse, for he'd sooner be d—d than run. Vot a valiant hidea!

NOKES. How did you sell him at all?

SAM. I'll tell you—I went into my stable one day, and I reasoned with the beast ; says I to him, "you brute! it's a waste of good hay and corn to give it you!" and I suppose my words affected his feelings, for he began kicking and prancing like them hanimals at Astley's. Vot a dramatic hidea!

NOKES. Well, the finish?

SAM. Just at this time, a indiwidual comes in, says he, "that's a spirited thing ; " "unkimmon," says I—"the price?" says he—"two hundred," says I ; there it is," says he—"thank you," says I ; and he gets a top of this dear bit of dog's meat, who, to my eternal surprise, gallops away ; that horse galloping as had never dewiated into a trot before. Vot a astonishing hidea!

NOKES. How long did his galloping last

SAM. Only to the end of the street.

NOKES. No!

SAM. No, he came to his senses again and stood as still as the monument.

NOKES. How do you account for all this?

SAM. Why, that's the critical pint , you see, this here hanimal in the early part of his life (for he was an old one) had been in the theatrical line, and at the time in question, a band of mouth-organ chaps was a playing ; (*whistles a tune.*) that was one of the tunes as he remembered hearing in his early days— off he goes, prancing along like a good one (as he was not,) but at the end of the street there was an end of the music, and he returned to his old ways.

NOKES. And so this came to a trial?

SAM. Summnut o' that sort—you know how they manages these things.

NOKES. A little.

SAM. But the judge was a ignorant, know-nothing hindividual, and I'm blest if he didn't call it swindling.

NOKES. Dreadful!

SAM. Warn't it?

NOKES. Well, a fine, I suppose—was that the finish?

SAM. No, Ned; for three blessed months I walked up stairs, and I never walked down again.

NOKES. The treadmill?

SAM. Yes; I took steps for altering my course of life. (*treads.*) Vot a fatiguing hidea!

NOKES. Why, I think you're thinner.

SAM. You think so; my broad shoulders and my stomach make my back look like the end of the Old Jewry.

NOKES. How do you mean?

SAM. Widened at the expense of the corporation. Vot a hanatomical hidea.

NOKES. Come, you'll do—you're in pretty good case yet.

SAM. No—skin and bone; my cup of misery isn't yet at its drregs. When I comed out of my confinement, my horses had walked off—my goods had walked off—my groom had walked off—

NOKES. And your wife—

SAM. Had walked off along with him.

NOKES. That's the finish?

SAM. It is; she started for Ameriky, and while I was on the stairs, (*treads.*), she was on the passage. Vot a harchitectural hidea! How's your master? (NOKES *shakes his head.*) Is he still of the light green shade?

NOKES. No; he begins to open his eyes; his ready's gone—his five thousand a-year dipped to about the tune of forty thousand—that's the finish.

SAM. In six months! vot a rapid hidea! I say, where do you hank? vot are you worth now—four thousand? Vot a hidea for a menial!

NOKES. I've been unlucky, too—I had saved a trifle, but—

SAM. But what?

NOKES. Do you remember an old coincidence about a gravy spoon or two, and a few silver forks, and some teapots, and other little things?

SAM. I begins to inwestigate the willany; privately stealing in a dwelling-house. Vot a burglarious hidea!

NOKES. They found me out.

SAM. No!

NOKES. Yes; and as I hate words, rather than go and explain it all away somewhere in—

SAM. Where?

NOKES. Newgate Street, where they wanted me to go—I gave—

SAM. How much?

NOKES. Three thousand pounds, and that's twelve times what the plate's worth, for I only sold it for two hundred and fifty pounds.

SAM. Then you did know summut about it? Vot, a fence—vhite soup, hey? vot a melting hidea!

NOKES. That ain't the finish!

SAM. No?

NOKES. No, there's a chap calls this compounding a felony, and comes to me twice a-month for hush-money.

SAM. Why, the himperent warmint! vot willians there is in the world, surely! Hush-money? vot a bribing hidea! Well, I say, what's to be done?—how's cash, eh?

NOKES. Why, I'm not stuck up for a canary or two.

(holding some sovereigns.

SAM. Canaries! the prettiest bird that flies. Canaries! vot a yellow hidea!

NOKES. I say, can't we, between us, contrive to mend matters a little.

SAM. They admits of it, certainly; your master's not plucked yet—and Mr. Markham—

NOKES. He's, as usual, in cash to-day—out to-morrow. But, come, I must raise the supplies.

SAM. Raise the supplies? Vot a parliamentary hidea! How's your present master off for plate, eh?

NOKES. That might be thought of.

SAM. I say, a door might be left open—promiscuous. Quite a haccidental hidea!

NOKES. If we join in anything like this, we must swear eternal friendship.

SAM. Till death! *(they look.)*

NOKES. That's a finish.

SAM. Vot a suspending hidea!   *Exeunt,* R.

SCENE III.—*A handsome Chamber, opening to Ball Room,* C.
(*3rd and 4th grooves.*) *Music without.*

Enter LADY BLAZON *and* FANNY, C.

LADY B. Retire to your own room, child?—not join our party!—positively, I will not hear of it. You have been a week in London, and haven't come out yet; not a soul have you seen, except your frowsy aunt, Mrs. Dabbleditch.

FANNY. My dear madam, my thoughts are ill fitted for gay scenes.

LADY B. What, is it melancholy, then? Why, child, if you are cold, do you not go to the fire? if you have been fatigued, do you not seek rest? and if you are sad, should you not seek merriment? Come, come, my dear, I must positively take you into a course of fashionable training.

FANNY. You will find me but a sorry pupil.

LADY B. Is its love away, and does it droop?

FANNY. Nay, this is unkind; you know I've other, and more serious causes for sorrow—if, indeed, what you allude to, be one at all.

LADY B. You cause for sorrow! my dear, you'll cost me a stay-lace. You are young, pretty, sing, dance well, know how to hear flattery, and how to answer it; take my word for it, dear, you have the best stock in hand with which to set up fortune making. Cause for sorrow! why, except me, my love, you haven't a friend to care for.

FANNY. Nor one that cares for me; many might think that alone an affliction.

LADY B. Not at all—quite the contrary! I never could discover the use of friends—they never send to one except when they want to be married or buried or some such thing—I say with the little man in the play—"Let me be happy and friend-less." But come now, you will join our party?

FANNY. I never was at a masked ball in my life.

LADY B. Then the more reason, dear, to see one now; but if you would rather be a pensive musing maid, join the promenade in this apartment, or the musicals in the next.

FANNY. Well, well, I will strive to be gay—I will endeavour to imitate your good humour.

LADY B. Very well, but you mustn't steal any of my beaux.

FANNY. You need not be alarmed. But who are they, may I ask?

LADY B. Oh, all the young fellows. Don't open those pretty eyes so wide—that's the priviledge of widowhood. When I was of your age, child, I was a good sort of yea-nay, open your eyes and shut your eyes, say nothing girl, but now I have passed the rubicon, I can flirt with one and toy with another—and the worst that folks say is—" That widow is such a strange creature."

FANNY. But in all this, Lady Blazon, what is there to touch the heart?

LADY B. The heart? Ha, ha, ha! My dear, I was born before hearts were invented. Poets call love a mighty ocean, and so it is ; but one may choose whether one plunges into the fathomless gulf, or dances on the light and fluttering spray.

Enter HARRY MARKHAM, C.

MARK. Partner for one for a waltz. Why, Lady Blazon, what are you about here? My dear Miss Moreland, you look—words for one ; I never could compliment in my life—but the reason is, that in this instance, what I ought to say far transcends anything that language allows.

FANNY. I see, Mr. Markham, satire, at least, is one of your qualifications.

MARK. Satire! no, on my honour—looking-glasses for one, and the fact will stare you in the face.

LADY B. Come, come, Mr. Markham, you forget I am present. But Miss Moreland is a new acquaintance, and poor I must sing willow.

MARK. Pray don't sing at all—everybody does it ; there's that fellow Fred Florid, screeching about the house till it's quite horrid. I wish they'd get gags for one.

LADY B. Do you dislike music?

MARK. Dislike music! astonishment for one enough for twenty. Look at me—am I a Goth? I doat on it, from the merry tang-tang of a coachman's horn to the gentle thrumming of a guitar ; but most I love the music of a woman's voice, when it comes in a gentle moonlight murmuring sort of melody, breathing of love and extacy—especially when it sings to me, and me alone.

LADY B. Why, Markham, you are getting sentimental.

MARK. Don't tell any of your friends so, they'll never believe you. But, come, merriment for two ; I'm for a waltz or gallopade.

LADY B. Have with you, then. Ha, ha, ha! what, you wanted Miss Moreland for a partner—but she don't dance, so you are compelled to have an old flame.

MARK. Don't dance! why everybody does it. *N'importe*—come, my dear widow ; I have foisted old Mrs. Dabbleditch upon poor Florid ; agony for one! let us go and enjoy his affliction.

LADY B. Come, then ; good bye, dear, I shall seek for you in the music room. Come, Markham. (*Music heard from ball room.*)   *Music.—They go off* C. *and* L.

FANNY. So, after all my resolution, I am in London, near him who vowed that my presence made up his existence, and now—no matter, no matter ; yet I little thought, six months since, when we parted for a day, that the parting was likely to be eternal.   *Exit* L.

(*the* COMPANY *are seen waltzing behind.*

MARKHAM *and* MRS. DABBLEDITCH *come forward—he waltzes her to a seat,* R.

MARK. (*aside.*) The deuce take that little witch of a widow, she has danced off with Florid herself, and left me with this old tabby.

MRS. D. Oh, Mr. Markham, the waltz is a most fatiguing dance, and rather indelicate.

MARK. Yes, ma'am—but everybody does it. (*aside.*) I hope she won't dance again.

MRS. D. A quadrille, now, is a much more elegant amusement.

MARK. Yes, ma'am, it may be very well for persons young and gay like yourself, but for me, in my delicate health, it's rather too much. Chairs for one.

MRS. D. Are you ill, Mr. Markham?

MARK. (*aside.*) Now she'll be fond, and that's worse. Yes, ma'am, very ill—sick.

MRS. D. Sick !

MARK (*aside.*) Yes, of you.

MRS. D. Oh, Mr. Markham, I fear you lead a very bad life.

MARK. Why, ma'am, I lead as bad a life as I can—a man can do no more. I must get rid of her. By-the-bye, have you seen Rakewell?—he's in the ball room ; he's a delightful fellow, and I know who he thinks a delightful woman.

MRS. D. Oh, Mr. Markham, you're so foolish.

MARK. Yes, there's two of us that way. I've heard him speak of you in terms—such terms, that I cannot repeat them. (*aside.*) That's true enough.

MRS. D. I must confess that Rakewell is a very fine young man.

MARK. Yes, ma'am ; constitution for two—spirits enough for twenty, and doats on you.

MRS. D. Now do you think so?

MARK. Don't I know so? (*aside.*) How she grins and exposes her remaining grinders ; she really ought to go to a dentist and get teeth for one.   Allow me to touch that delicate hand.   Hoofs for one, and fetlocks to follow.

Music.—They go off through arch, R.

Enter LADY BLAZON *and* RAKEWELL, *through arch, from* L.

LADY B. (R. C.) Come, come, Mr. Rakewell, there is something weighing upon your spirits.

RAKE. Oh, a trifle ; out a few thousands at the first spring meeting, and at the moment it was inconvenient; but your smiles would recall a Timon from his melancholy.

LADY. B. My smiles! no, no, Mr. Rakewell, you young heirs meet with too much sunshine to care for a solitary ray, though from a source which would shed its beams for you, and you alone. *(aside.)* He is a nice fellow, and certainly rich.

RAKE. You wrong us, at least, you wrong me—I am already sick of what they call pleasure ; I go to races, balls, plays, masquerades, till my very senses ache with the exhaustion of what they tell me is delight.   But ah! I'm not half so happy as when I rose with the lark, mounted old Dobbin, and galloped over to Moreland's house—hey, d—n it! I mustn't think that way.   Come, widow, shall we be gay—will you engage me at *écarté?*

LADY B. You think of nothing but play, Rakewell.

RAKE. (C.) Oh yes, of much beside.

LADY B. Do you? may one guess what?

RAKE. Of love when I am beside you.

LADY B. Come, come, this is quite too good.

RAKE. Nay, believe me—by this fair hand! this slender waist! those ruddy lips! (*kisses her.*)

LADY B. Mr. Rakewell, you forget where you are, sir, and who I am.

RAKE. Forgive me, dear Lady Blazon—attribute it to an ardent passion ; let me plead for pardon on my knees.   I love you—

Enter FANNY, L.

FANNY. My dear Lady Blazon, I come to—

RAKE. Fanny Moreland!

FANNY. Rakewell, I was not prepared for this—I will retire.

RAKE. No, no—Fanny, I conjure you, stay.

LADY B. Ah! very well, Mr. Rakewell, I compliment you on your sincerity and gentleman-like attention.   I shall however, find my way to the music-room unattended ; I wouldn't interrupt your *tête-a-tête* for the the world.   Miss Moreland, your very humble servant.   *Exit,* C. *to* R.

FANNY. Lady Blazon—madam—I beg—

RAKE. No, no, Fanny.

FANNY. Sir! we must be strangers henceforth, Mr. Rakewell. (*aside.*) And I must teach my tongue these accents.

RAKE. Fanny, I have been guilty, very guilty—but I love you.

FANNY. I heard you say as much to Lady Blazon, but now.

RAKE. That was the passion of the moment.

FANNY. And this—

RAKE. Has been my solace for years.

FANNY. No, Rakewell, no; six months have passed since we last met.   Have you once thought of your Fanny—once written? No.   Tear after tear dewed my cheek—anxious fears were checked by ardent hope, till hope itself felt faint at my heart, and I felt you had forgotten me!

RAKE. No, not forgotten, Fanny.

FANNY. Only neglected! Rakewell, I cannot bear that from you!

RAKE. If you knew the temptations and pleasures that surrounded me—

FANNY. Did you know the troubles and miseries that surrounded me! Hear me, Rakewell—ere my father died, when I was rich and you poor, you were my heart's choice; fortune changed, but I was still the same—how was it with you? Had you been a beggar, Rakewell, I would have shared existence with you, and never felt a sorrow till you lacked a joy; but now my soul turns from you with loa— No, not with loathing; I forgive you, man—may Heaven forgive you too!

Exit C., *and* R.

RAKE. 'Sdeath! I— Yet, do I not deserve it? When I was friendless, I was all to her—and six months have passed, and I have lost thousands—more, I have lost her! Wine—wine!

(goes to table R.

Enter MARKHAM, *through arch from* R.

MARK. So say I—wine for two. (*sits* L., *of table.*) Hallo! what's the matter, Tom?—you are in pain.

RAKE. Yes, here.

MARK. The heart!—the only place I never have a pain in.

RAKE. I'm mad!

MARK. Mad!—strait waistcoats for one.

RAKE. I can't stay here—let's go.

MARK. Ah, let's leave this dull place, and be off to Crockford's.

RAKE. No; I'm too much out already.

MARK. And may you not be twice as much in? Bad luck to-day, better to-morrow; the rain must clear at last, however strong the storm.

RAKE. True—come to Crockford's—anywhere, for I'm mad. Come! *Exeunt L.*

Enter MRS. DABBLEDITCH *and* FANNY, C. *from* R.

MRS. D. The men are all brutes!—and as to the women, they're— No matter. Fanny, my dear, you shall not stay here any longer; you shall come home with me, child. We are too mild and patient to deal with these people. You tell me you have been ill-used—I know I have been ill-used—and we'll go and weep in secret. Oh, I should like to be revenged on the whole set! Come, child come. *Exeunt L.*

SCENE IV.—*A Street.* (*2nd grooves.*) *Moonlight. Lights down.* •

Enter NOKES, L.

NOKES. I never was so poor since I took to living upon other people. A ten pound note, and that's the finish; and I don't know how long that may be mine. There's that rascal, Snump, who threatens to peach—if he comes, all's up. So, master's been to Crockford's, has met Sam, and now gone somewhere worse. He's a going it. I hope Sam will look out. If he robs master, I suppose he'll behave honourable to me—if not, I'll peach. Talk of the devil—there's Snump.

Enter SNUMP, R.

SNUMP. C'up.

NOKES. Don't bawl. What do you mean by cup?

SNUMP. Tip.

NOKES. That's the finish!

SNUMP. Quick.

NOKES. (*aside.*) If I give him this ten pound note, he'll never give me any change out. (*aloud.*) I haven't a shilling, if you'll believe me.

SNUMP. I don't.

NOKES. Wait till daylight.

SNUMP. I won't. (*going.*)

NOKES. What are you going to do?

SNUMP. Peach.

NOKES. That's the finish! Stop—there's a ten pound note; give me back five.

SNUMP. No.

NOKES. Two?

SNUMP. No.

NOKES. I only want a trifle to get some refreshment.

SNUMP. Oh! (*gives four halfpence.*)

NOKES. What's this?

SNUMP. Two pence.

NOKES. What'll this get?

SNUMP. A pint of beer—many an honest hard-working man can't get that.

NOKES. But I'm not a hard-working man.

SNUMP. No—nor honest.

NOKES. What a thief you are to what I am.

SNUMP. Am I?

NOKES. You're an informer!

SNUMP. I know it.

NOKES. Arn't you ashamed?

SNUMP. Not a bit—if every thief had an informer to dog him, there would be few thieves.

NOKES. But you don't do it from a good motive.

SNUMP. Yes I do.

NOKES. What?

SNUMP. To feed the poor.

NOKES. The poor?

SNUMP. Myself and family. I haven't the courage to be a thief, nor you the courage to meet a thief's doom.

NOKES. How long do you mean to follow me in this way?

SNUMP. While you live.

NOKES. I'll kill myself.

SNUMP. You haven't the courage.

NOKES. I'll kill you.

SNUMP. You haven't the strength.

NOKES. I'll go to America.

SNUMP. I'll not let you.

NOKES. That's the finish—you know I can't keep you for ever.

SNUMP. I shan't live for ever.

NOKES. Ah, then when you die—

SNUMP. My son will follow you—he knows you.

NOKES. Ha! what shall I do?

SNUMP. Submit.

NOKES. You'll never die in your bed.

SNUMP. I don't expect it.

NOKES. Where then?

SNUMP. In yours—you'll pay for my bed as long as you live. Good morning.

NOKES. Ah, you are going.

SNUMP. I shall see you again in a day or two.   *Exit*, R.

NOKES. That fellow's got no conscience. I wonder what Sam's got out of master? Oh, you herring-gutted villain!

That fellow's my fetch.   A sneaking cowardly rascal!—a man that would peach, would do anything.   If Sam don't come down handsomely, I'll inform against him, as sure as my name is Ned Nokes.   *Exit*, L.

SCENE V.—*A Gaming House.*   (*3rd grooves.*)   *Table, three chairs, dice, &c.*

MARKHAM, RAKEWELL, *and* SAM *discovered, seated.*

SAM. (L.) All cleaned out—vot a pleasant hidea!

RAKE. (C.) The devil was in the dice.

MARK. (R.) Something was in the dice, for I'll swear they were loaded.

RAKE. 'Sdeath! if I thought so, I'd—

SAM. It is no use—they're all off—no one but the porter, and he's deaf.

RAKE. What induced you, Hal, to get me in at chickin hazard? Chicken hazard! a pretty name! why do they call it so?

MARK. Chicken hazard! because there's so much foul play in it. Sam, call a coach.

SAM. I will.   I say, have either of you—hey?

RAKE. Not a rap.   Hal—

MARK. The same here.

SAM. Vot a hidea! three respectable hindividuals, and not a rap among us.   I've a ticker—I'm off to my uncle's.

RAKE. What does he mean?

MARK. Everybody does it.

SAM. Quite a common hidea.   I'll get a coach—wot a rumbling hidea!   *Exit*, L.

RAKE. Hal, you see a ruined man.

MARK. I see two.

RAKE. What's to be done?

MARK. Marry.

RAKE. Who?

MARK. Mother Dabbleditch.

RAKE. Faugh!

MARK. She has a hundred thousand pounds.

RAKE. Had she millions, I would not wed the wretch.

Enter NED NOKES, L.

How did you find us out here?

NOKES. Instinct, sir.   A letter—that's the finish!

RAKE. Very apropos—from the old harridan.   A pressing invitation for a morning visit.   There's her scrawl.

MARK. What a sweet hand for a check.

RAKE. Ned, Mr. Markham and I have been unfortunate at play—what money have you?

NOKES. Two-pence, sir.

RAKE. &
MARK. } Two-pence!

NOKES. Not a rap more, as I'm a Christian.

RAKE. I can't endure all this.

Enter SAM, L.

SAM. Coach is ready.

RAKE. Come.

MARK. Where?

RAKE. To Mrs. Dabbleditch—to the devil—come.

Exit RAKEWELL, and MARKHAM, L.

SAM. I say, Ned, there's your share of the last swag ; and see —though I've stuck up my ticker, it's in the family still. Vot a knowing hidea! (*shows the watch, which he had only concealed.*

Exeunt L.

SCENE VI.—*A Front Chamber. 2nd grooves.*)—*Lights up.*

Enter BETTY and PEGGY, R.

BETTY. Oh, I'm in such a bustle! it can't be true! Mr. Rakewell now with your mistress! that old frumpy dumpy, huffy, snuffy, old wretch!

PEGGY. What do you mean by calling her a wretch?

BETTY. Why, you called her so yourself just now.

PEGGY. That may be. I don't mind her being called a wretch, but I don't like to be called a wretch's waiting-woman.

BETTY. She marry that nice, dear, sweet—no, he is a nasty false, perfidy, roystering, racketing rascal, that he is. Oh, I'm in such a bustle! this was the end of Mrs. Dabbleditch's kindness, was it? Invite her poor neice to her house to steal her husband from her! I should like to see anyone take a man from me, that's all! But I'll go and pack up my trunk—

PEGGY. Here comes my missus.

BETTY. Does she? Oh, I'm in such a bustle! If I don't tell her a bit of my mind, I'm no woman. A squinty, flinty, jeering, leering old fool. Oh, I am in such a bustle!

Exeunt, L.

Enter MARKHAM, RAKEWELL, and MRS. DABBLEDITCH, R.

MARK. (L.) Steady, my boy! staggers for one.

MRS. D. (R.) Oh, you insinuating wretch! this morning it cannot be. (*turning up stage*, R.)

RAKE. (C.) Thank heaven!

MARK. For what?

RAKE. You hear. She says it cannot be.

MARK. What of that?

RAKE. I can't do this, Hal—I love another.

MARK. Of course—everybody does it. Husband for one, love for two, liking for ever so many.

RAKE. My spirit cannot brook it.

MARK. Ruin!

RAKE. 'Twill break Fanny Moreland's hear..

MARK. Ruin!

RAKE. No, no—welcome poverty.

MARK. That's not all—debts of honour unpaid.

RAKE. Death and damnation! then I must do it.

MARK. I have the license—signatures for two.

Enter BETTY *and* FANNY, L.

FANNY. (L.) Dear aunt, I come—Rakewell?

BETTY. (L. C.) Forgive me, Miss—I dared not tell you. There stands Mr. Thomas Rakewell, that used to come late and early to look upon you! there's a man selling himself for lucre to to that old frumpy humpy woman.

MRS. D. (R.) Ah!

FANNY. Betty, she is my aunt.

BETTY. I don't care—she ain't mine. I say it's a shame—a burning shame! to leave a beautiful young creature like you for that old daub.

MRS. D. Old daub!

BETTY. Because one is poor, and the other rich. (*goes up*, L.)

MARK. My dear everybody does it.   (*goes up*, L. C.)

RAKE. Fanny, hear me!

FANNY. Stand off, sir! you have deceived—do not insult me.

RAKE. (C.) Hold! I will—

MARK. (R. C.) No, he won't, indeed—he never does—

RAKE. Villain!

MARK. You see, he don't know what he says—he calls me a villian.

FANNY. I did not think our eyes would ever meet again. Go, Rakewell—I free you from your vows. Now, worlds could not make you mine—were you more wealthy than even my fondest wishes would have made you, more dear than my heart deemed you. The dream is over! on earth we meet no more. May we live so as to hope to meet hereafter. (*throws herself on* BETTY'S neck, L. C.—*picture.*)

END OF ACT II.

ACT III.

SCENE I.—*A Chamber.* (*1st grooves.*)

Enter LADY BLAZON and MARTHA, R.

LADY B. Hasn't John returned yet?

MARTHA. No, ma'am; I don't think he'll come back any more.

LADY B. What do you mean?

MARTHA. Why, ma'am, John ain't had no wages of you for eighteen months, and when he left home, to-day, he threatened to apply to a magistrate.

LADY B. To a magistrate? for what?

MARTHA. To see if the law allowed fashionable people to withold from their servants their hard earned wages.

LADY B. I never heard anything so infamous in my life; what an exposure among my fashionable friends!

MARTHA. Oh, don't fret, ma'am; several of your ladyship's friends are in the same situation.

LADY B. What's to be done? Was the letter sent to Lord Looby?

MARTHA. Yes, ma'am; he's abroad.

LADY B. What answer from Sir Charles?

MARTHA. He's in the Fleet.

LADY B. From Sir Jessamy Jinks?

MARTHA. He's in the Bench.

LADY B. Mr. Markham?

MARTHA. He's there, too.

LADY B. What shall I do? If I could meet any enterprising young man, I'd have him, if he came pennyless to me; he would at least release me from a load of liabilities. It's a thousand pities I didn't secure young Rakewell.

MARTHA. Oh, ma'am he's nearly as bad off as t'others.

LADY B. Thus, then, end all my splendid visions! and, of the many that shared in the gaieties, follies, and frivolities of this mansion, not one is to be found to alleviate its solitude and sorrow! (*crossing to* R.)

MARTHA. Ma'am!

LADY B. Well?

MARTHA. Would it be quite convenient to you to pay me my wages?

LADY B. You know I cannot.

MARTHA. Then, I must take something to the value.

LADY B. You would not dare do it?

MARTHA. Yes, I would. I shall only take what I've worked for, and, if I do wrong, you are now as poor as myself, therefore you'll get none to redress you.

LADY B. What a base wretch you are! You don't consider my feelings.

MARTHA. Did you ever consider mine? When riches poured upon you, you were proud, harsh, and cruel. *I* felt it then, and *you* shall feel the effects of it now.

LADY B. Leave me, ungrateful girl!

MARTHA. What have I to be grateful for? You never gave me a gown until the fashion made it impossible that you should ever wear it again, and then it was wrung from you by flattery, which I despise myself for uttering, and you for listening to. But I can't stand talking to you; I must pack up my things and go, for I suppose there won't be a chair to sit upon to-morrow. I'm sure—fine ladies not paying their servants—it's quite a shame—so it is.   *Exit,* L.

LADY B. This is the severest blow of all! it has wrung my very heart. Oh, if ever I recover fortune again, I'll make that hussey suffer for this!

Re-enter MARTHA.

MARTHA. There's a man wants you.

LADY B. What man?

MARTHA. I can't be troubled running up and down stairs for you; there he is, ask him yourself. This way, Mr. Thingamy.
                                                     Exit, L.

Enter BRIGGS.

BRIGGS. I'm very sorry, Lady Blazon, but I've an account against you. In plain words, you are my prisoner.

LADY B. At whose suit?

BRIGGS. Two; Mr. Wokley, the upholsterer, three thousand two hundred; Mr. Osrick, the jeweller, one thousand eight hundred.

LADY B. I'll send to some of my friends for bail.

BRIGGS. Won't do—they are Ca. Sa's. Allow me, madam.

LADY B. I shall faint!

BRIGGS. This way, ma'am.

LADY B. I must see some of my friends.

BRIGGS. My house, ma'am, is as likely a place to see your friends as any I know   *Exeunt* L.

SCENE II.—*The King's Bench.* (4*th grooves.*) *The room divided by a curtain. Bed,* L., *in which* MARKHAM *is discovered. Table and chair,* R., *cup with dice, and plate with chop, on table.*

Enter RAKEWELL *and* TURNKEY, R.

TURNKEY. This is your room, sir.

RAKE. This!

TURNKEY. This half of it; t'other side belongs to the gentleman you're chumm'd upon; but you'll find him quite a gentleman, I assure you, and you'll be as happy as the day is long.

Exit, R.

RAKE. (*sitting,* R.) This, then, is the end of all my follies! Oh, Markham!—Harry Markham, all this I owe to your pernicious counsel!

MARK. (*in bed,* L.) Hollo! quiet for one; none of your tricks, Jenks.

RAKE. That voice—Harry!

MARK. Hollo! (*looking through curtain.*) Tom Rakewell!—room for two!—when did you render?

RAKE. But this moment.

MARK. I've been here a month, and a very snug place it is; come into my room—I want to have some talk with you.

RAKE. Your room?

MARK. Yes, my room; they divide them, here—everybody does it. This is not quite so gay as your villa, in Twickenham; saw it advertised for sale by Robins. What did it fetch?

RAKE. I know not.

MARK. I see; sold for the benefit of your creditors. Well, I am quite dished—I suppose you have a few cool hundreds in a snug corner?

RAKE. I have not ten pounds in the world.

MARK. Ten pounds!—have you five? lend me a couple— (RAKEWELL *gives two.*) everybody does it. A dressing gown for one, and slippers to follow. (*gets up.*) Upon second thoughts, Tom, two pounds are no use to me, nor three to you—let's throw for them.

RAKE. No, hang the dice, I hate them.

MARK. I've heard you say that, often! what, you're going to shut the stable door now the horse is stolen!—come.

RAKE. Well, where are the dice? (MARKHAM *shews the cup* —RAKEWELL *throws.*) Seven!

MARK. (*throws.*) Sixes!—you're nicked; this is opening the bank strong this morning.

RAKE. Now I'm without a shilling! (*crosses to* L.)

MARK. (R.) Don't droop—I'll lend you some. I'll go and have a touch at hazard, below. Have you dined?

RAKE. No.

MARK. Here's a mutton chop and bread; you'll find pepper and salt in the cupboard to follow; I'll send you some porter from the tap.

RAKE. I see you're still the same, Hal.

MARK. Yes—I don't change, though my coats do, cursedly.
(*going*, R.

NOKES. (*without*, R.) That's my master's room—No. 6 in 7.

RAKE. Six in seven! what does that mean?

MARK. Why we are all at sixes and sevens, here. (NOKES *speaks again, and* MARKHAM *jumps into bed.*)

Enter MRS. DABBLEDITCH, R.

MRS. D. Wretch! see what you've come to.

MARK. Oh, a woman!—I thought it was Nat Graves come for his bill; how d'ye do, ma'am?

MRS. D. A man—and a-bed too; how indelicate!

MARK. Not at all, ma'am; everybody does it.

MRS. D. Oh, it's you, Mr. Markham, is it?

MARK. I see—a row for one—I'm off. I shall try my luck with the bones. Good bye, ma'am—I'll send you some porter from the tap—use my room without any ceremony—famous place for a curtain lecture.   *Exit*, R.

MRS. D. Oh, wretch! see what you've brought me to; all my fortune lavished away, and not even solaced by the little endearments that render sorrow endurable! where is my money?

RAKE. Gone.

MRS. D. My houses?

RAKE. Sold.

MRS. D. My jewels?

RAKE. Pawned.

MRS. D. What, my ornaments—the gems that threw a charm on my beauty!—oh, it is too much! (*cries.*)

RAKE. Peace, woman!—weep not for the gauds of a girl. Is this a time for selfish sorrow? I am wrung, head and heart! I have lost a jewel nothing can restore.

MRS. D. What?

RAKE. Peace of mind, and purity of heart, gone and gone from me for ever. (*crosses to* R.)

MRS. D. Ungrateful wretch! to whom I gave my fond affections—oh, "Let lovely woman beware how she listens to the voice of the charmer, charm he never so wisely." What am I to do? I can't live without attendants—equipage—household—and I won't—that's flat.

RAKE. Oh, Fanny Moreland! how unlike you is this.

MRS. D. Fanny Moreland! how dare you insult me by naming her?

BOY. (*without*, R.) Beer!

Enter BOY, R.

Gentleman ordered a pot of beer.

MRS. D. Pot of beer! how indelicate!

RAKE. 'Twas Markham—leave it.

BOY. I can't leave it without the money.

RAKE. 'Sdeath! and I have not a shilling in the world! Go.

BOY. Go! no go, I think! Pretty gentleman—can't pay for a pot of beer! *Exit*, R.

RAKE. I wonder that I am not mad.

MRS. D. You ought to be, when you think what you have brought me to.

RAKE. Peace, woman!—let me not hear your raven voice.

MRS. D. My raven voice!—the brute's mad to a certainty. I'll not remain with him—I've a relation in Hampshire—I'll go outside the Portsmouth mail. Mail did I say!—I'll have nothing to do with the filthy male again. That your miseries may every day grow greater, till you awake to a sense of the wrongs done my susceptible heart, is my last and earnest wish. You brute! *Exit* R.

RAKE. Ned!

Enter NOKES, R.

NOKES. Any commands, sir?

RAKE. Ned, you have been long a faithful follower of mine; it pains me to say it, but I'm unable any longer to support a servant—you must seek your fortune elsewhere. Ah! can I live through this!

(RAKEWELL *throws himself on bed, scene closes.*

SCENE III.—*Racket Ground.* (*2nd grooves.*)

Enter NOKES, L., *meeting* SNUMP, R.

NOKES. Snump, you have been long a faithful follower of mine; it grieves me to say it—Walker!—but I can no longer support you—you must seek your fortune elsewhere.

SNUMP. I won't.

NOKES. You won't?

SNUMP. No—I'll stick by you till death.

NOKES. But I'm out of place—I can't work for you.

SNUMP. Then steal for me.

NOKES. But why should I—you're no relation of mine?

SNUMP. If I was, you wouldn't relieve me. I think you've a mother, haven't you?

NOKES. I have.

SNUMP. Now, during your career with Rakewell, what have you ever sent her?

NOKES. Nothing.

SNUMP. What a fine specimen of manhood you are ; natural love has never extracted a shilling—unmanly fear has cost you ¬undreds.

NOKES. Snump—stump!—I'll have no preachy and floggy too—and that's the finish. Hollo !

Enter SAM, R.

SAM. It is the werry individual! Ned Nokes caged at last! Vot a confined hidea !

NOKES. Why, Sam, I shouldn't have known you!—how you are altered.

SAM. For the worser?

NOKES. Rather.

SAM. Who's that individual?

NOKES. Oh, that's my fetch.

SAM. What—the peaching varmint—the man of information? Vot a common hidea!

NOKES. Sam, speak to him—bluster it a little.

SAM. I will. (*crosses to* c.) I say, old bacco-pipe, I wonder you can look an honest man in the face?

SNUMP. I don't.

SAM. Vot a cantankerous hidea! You are just sich a villain as would rob a church.

SNUMP. And you, a churchyard.

SAM. Vot a body-snatching hidea! Vy, Ned, he knows me.

SNUMP. Yes, I do ; did you never hocus a horse at Epsom ?

SAM. Hocus ?—vot a poisoning idea !

SNUMP. C'up !

NOKES. That's the finish. Dub up, Sam, or you'll never get rid of him.

SAM. There's half a crown. (*aside.*) It's a bad one—vot a smashing hidea !

SNUMP. (*putting his hand to* SAM's *waistcoat.*) Do you deal in these ?

SAM. Leave off tickling a fellow there.

SNUMP. You'll be tickled up higher some of these times. (*taking another half-crown from* SAM'S *pocket.*) I shall mark these and keep them as evidence.

SAM. Evidence!—vot a legal hidea! Come, there's a good one. (*offering half-crown.*)

SNUMP. I must have a sovereign now.

SAM. I ain't got it.

SNUMP. A lie!

SAM. I can't get it.

SNUMP. Another.

SAM. Calls a gentlemen a liar. Vot a haggravating hidea!

SNUMP. (*crosses to* R.) I'll show these to the marshall.

SAM. (*crosses to* C.) Stop! there's the ready—(*gives a sovereign.*) and now be off with you, for the sight of you gives me a pain just here. Vot a unpleasant hidea! (*goes up.*)

SNUMP. (*to* NED.) C'up!

NOKES. I've only a few shillings.

SNUMP. I'll have them.

NOKES. There! (*emptying purse.*) That's the finish.

SNUMP. Good bye; I shall see you both to-morrow. *Exit,* R.

SAM. Vot a kind hidea! that is a vagabond, surely.

NOKES. Sam, what brought you here?

SAM. I'm a prisoner, bless you.

NOKES. What for?

SAM. Only for telling a lie.

NOKES. Telling a lie?

SAM. Yes, I promised to pay a man and I didn't. Vot a creditable hidea! But I say, Ned, is it all up? no go, no how? couldn't we do something together?

NOKES. Are you willing?

SAM. I am, and I arn't particular; I've gone on day by day, year by year—getting, I may say, worser and worser, and now I stick at nothing—only I'd rather prefer doing summut for which, if found out, they couldn't hurt us above the armpits.

NOKES. You know Miss Fanny Moreland—she has a hundred a-year—principal money—about two thousand four hundred, now lies at Coutts's.

SAM. I see—a forgery—vot a literary hidea!

NOKES. Come to the tap and we'll talk it over—it must be done directly; you can write it, I'll utter it.

SAM. (*crosses to* R.) That's kind! now, how beautiful it is to see two men, like you and I, trying to assist one another. Come what will, Ned, through thick and thin, we'll hang together. (NED *starts.*) Well, so we will—nothing's done without friendship and combination. Vot a co-operative hidea!

Exeunt, L.

Enter MARKHAM, *with a letter and bank notes*, R.

MARK. Devilish lucky that Sir Flashly O'Flynn, who levanted after last Leger should have turned up a trump at last.   This windfall was wanted, and I am a free man; now for Tom's letter once more. *(reading.)* " Scoundrel—insulted—Fanny—innocence—know you to be a villian—want only my liberty to prove you a coward."   This is a trifle too much, Master Rakewell—I've paid your debts, and by this time your discharge is at the gate and my challenge in your hand—attend it, and I'll prove that though I may be a villain, at least I am not a coward.   *Exit* L.

SCENE IV.—*The Heath.*   *(4th grooves.)*   *Moonlight.*
Lights down.
Enter RAKEWELL, R. U. E.

RAKE. 'Tis past the hour, and yet he does not come ; will he not come ?   No, I know him too well to doubt that.   Fanny ! my own, my beautiful Fanny ! deserted by him she doated on, and left to the mercy of a libertine.   What will be the issue ? I shall murder my friend, the partner of my boyhood's sports, my manhood's follies—or he murders me.   Well, welcome the worst—the worst is death, and that I pray for.

Enter MARKHAM, L. U. E., *with a case of pistols.*

MARK. An adversary for one ; is that you ?
RAKE. It is.   Harry Markham, you are a villain !
MARK. What?
RAKE. A perjured villain !   Recall our early days, sir.   My arm was your aid—my purse your banker.
MARK. Granted.
RAKE. How was this repaid ?   You decoyed me, drunk, into a marriage with a wretch, and when you put it beyond my power to right my Fanny, strove to wrong her.
MARK. Everybody does it.
RAKE. Man, I come not here to jest.
MARK. Nor I—I come to fight.   I am what the world has made me ; it found me guileless, and left me heartless.   I may be a villain, a scoundrel, a gamester, but I don't choose to be called so.   You have added coward, that word your life only can repair ; take your choice. *(offering pistols.)*
RAKE. Your blood be on your own head.

MARK. Your hand, old fellow ; I bear you no malice, but I'll blow you into eternity with all the pleasure in life—my honour demands it.   If I should happen to shoot you, I have horses for one behind the hedge ; if I fall, do you mount ; it's no use for either of us to be transported about a woman.

RAKE. Peace, villain—she's an angel.

MARK. Well, I dare say she is ; but if I go, the odds are, it won't be where angels are to be met with, so you needn't be jealous.   Come, take your ground, and when I give the word, fire.   Are you ready ?

RAKE. Quite.

MARK. Fire. (*they fire*—HARRY *falls.*)

RAKE. Ha!

MARK. I'm dished.

RAKE. Speak, Harry Markham, speak !

MARK. It's all up.   Fly, Tom, fly, and good fortune, my boy— Ha, ha !   your hand was so d——d unsteady, the bullet took a zigzag direction.

RAKE. Courage, man, it can't be fatal !

MARK. It is, Tom, it is ;   you are the first man that ever touched my heart. (*clapping his hand on the wound.*)   Mark my dying words—don't bet on the Sandford race, it's a done thing —hedge, if you have—ha, ha !   A coffin for one—and a tombstone to follow. (*dies—scene closes.*)

————

SCENE V.—*A Chamber.*   (*2nd grooves.*)   *Lights up.*

Enter FANNY, R.

FANNY. Still no news of him for whom I have sacrificed my life, and now friendless and unprotected I am left to the persecution of a libertine.   Poverty, poverty !   your greatest curse is, that you expose your victims to the insults of the vulgar rich, and the fashionably vicious.

Enter BETTY, L.

BETTY. I'm in such a bustle.   Oh, Miss Fanny !   Miss Fanny, there's been a man here to say that your banker has been cheated out of all your money, and that you haven't a penny in the world.

FANNY. Heaven forgive the heart that could rob a friendless orphan.

BETTY. Forgive him !   I'm in such a bustle ;   I never did see an execution, but when that fellow's catched, hang me if I don't.

FANNY. Hush, Betty, you do not know the temptations that may have led to the crime.

BETTY. And he doesn't care for the miseries that follow it. I am in such a bustle ; look here, miss, a good-looking creature like me works hard for the mere means of keeping life and soul together—if I was to do anything wrong, what a hullaballoo there'd be ; then what excuse is there for a lord of the creation, who uses his strength for our undoing, and then pleads his own weakness as an excuse for his crime ?

FANNY. Tell me, Betty, have you heard any more of Rakewell ?

BETTY. I left the letter at the house, ma'am—but he's gone away.

FANNY. Gone away?

BETTY. Gone to gaol ; yes, the nasty, perfidy, good-for-nothing fellow—and too good for him. Ah, if I had my will, he should be kept for twenty years on bread and water—and very little of that.

FANNY. Peace!

BETTY. Cruel! false! selfish!

FANNY. Peace, I tell you.

BETTY. La, miss! I only spoke out of regard for you.

FANNY. Those who regard me, mustn't slander him. Oh, my own, my first love! dearer are you to me in misery than even in your proudest day. A thousand recollections of kindness—a thousand memories of happiness come with the mention of his name! Leave me, Betty.

BETTY. Oh, Miss Moreland, it cuts me to the heart to hear you say so ; I'm sure I always said that Mr. Rakewell was a sweet young gentleman till he married that nasty old frowsy—

FANNY. Peace, woman! his wife claims my respect. Never again let your tongue utter one word against poor Tom Rakewell ; if he has been guilty, I am the sufferer, and I can suffer and be still—but now, when misery lays heavy on him, is it a time for reproach ? Fly to him, Betty—bear him this note, it may alleviate his wants, it cannot mine.

BETTY. Oh, miss, miss! do forgive me ; I arn't such a flinty hearted wretch, neither—what can I do?—I am in such a bustle! (going-off, L., and returning with a box.) Here's all I've saved in your and your dear father's service ; take every penny of it—I'd rather starve myself, and beg for you, than think that any one you loved wanted a meal.

FANNY. Oh, Betty, Betty!   (embraces her—scene closes.

SCENE VI.—*A Street.* (*1st grooves.*)

Enter SAM, NOKES, SNUMP, *and* OFFICER, R.

SAM. (*entering.*) Taken up for a forgery! Vy vot a hidea.

OFFICER. It appears a clear case.

SNUMP. Very!

SAM. Vy now, look rationally at this here. Suppose I did write that bit of paper, vy vot of that?—in the hurry of the moment a man may sign another gentleman's name by mistake, mayn't he, sir?—vot a confused hidea!

SNUMP. No; besides, this was a lady's name.

SAM. When a man's in a hurry, he hardly knows whether he's a lady or a gentleman. Vot a neuter hidea!

OFFICER. The case is clear enough—you were seen to write it.

SNUMP. I'll prove that.

OFFICER. (*to* NOKES.) And you to utter it.

SNUMP. And that, too.

OFFICER. Any jury in the world would find you guilty.

SAM. Ned, we shall be hung.

NOKES. That's the finish!

OFFICER. No; the wisdom of our rulers has lately blended mercy with justice; your lives will be spared, but they will be passed in a distant land.

SAM. Vot a transporting hidea!

SNUMP. I shall come and see you at the hulks.

NOKES. You're very good, I'm sure.

OFFICER. Come!

SAM. Vich is the vay to Newgate Street?

Exeunt SAM, NOKES, *and* OFFICER, L.

SNUMP. When they are both transported, I shall be a little more comfortable! I'll go and see 'em locked up.   *Exit,* L.

———

SCENE VII.—*The Madhouse.—Half dark.* (*4th grooves.*)
Door, R. 3 E., *and window,* L. C.

RAKEWELL *discovered, amid the straw, and chained to a post,* R.

RAKE. I wonder if 'tis day or night?—I know no change in either. Day comes to me without its sunshine, and night without its star. They tell me I am mad!—yes, here, here, at my heart. If I am mad, they should pity, not torture me; they chain me as a beast, and wonder that I am become like one. I'm left alone—all alone in this dreary solitude; I'll not bear it—I will, I will be free! I'll rend—I'll—ha! ha! ha! (*pulling violently at the chains, sinks by the post, exhausted.*) Ha! vain—'tis all in vain! (*rises.*) I have a sense of deadly wrong, though I do not know my wrongers—I feel 'tis they who keep me—'tis they that torture thus!—I'm a wretched, naked man, within their thrall, and thus they treat me! I'll not endure it. I know that there is strength within this little arm to rend a sphere asunder; and I will—I will—will be free. (*struggling again with chain, it breaks.*) Ha, ha, ha! (*rushes to front, and falls.*) Free again!—again free—now for vengeance—this shall be my weapon. (*lifting chain.*) I'll rush among them—I'll scale the wall. (*ascends the wall, and clutches the bars,* L. C.—FANNY *sings without—he jumps down.*) That voice—it pierces through my heart—my brain—how well I know that voice! Why come they not now? I'm calm—why do they leave me thus alone, where all is cold—cold—all cold—but here, and here, all is fire!

(*the door is heard to unlock—*RAKEWELL, *who is kneeling, rushes back to the post,* R., *and attempts to re-fasten his chain.*)

Enter KEEPER, D. R. 3 E.—*comes down—beckons on* FANNY.

KEEPER. Now you may speak with safety.

RAKE. (*stealing towards* FANNY.) Hush!

FANNY. My heart will break! Rakewell, do you not know me?

RAKE. (*looking towards* KEEPER.) Hush! (FANNY *beckons to* KEEPER. *who crosses to* R.) I know you well. (*whispers.*)

FANNY. Do you not know my name?

RAKE. I have forgotten that.

FANNY. Hear me, Rakewell—my father's fortune is restored to me, and I shall, indeed, be happy, if I can make you so.

RAKE. Now *you* are mad—know you not I'm married?

FANNY. She is dead; and her last prayer was for your forgiveness.

RAKE. We should all forgive, for we all lack much of forgiveness. Oh! memory gushes in torrents on my brain. I know all now—I know you well, though I do not know your name! Bear with me a little, and I will know it—nay, do not tell me—it is—it is—(*after a great struggle.*) Fanny! Fanny! Fanny! (*kneeling and clasping* FANNY, *weeping.*)

FANNY. Oh! restrain those tears.

RAKE. Check them not—tears are the blessed waters of the soul, that flow to purify it. But I'll be calm—I'll not rave

again; indeed I will not. I do remember—I am he who had
lost a fortune! my mother is in the cold grave—my father, too,
he sleeps the long sleep! I tarry yet, the worst for me; my
mind is in it's grave.

FANNY. Doubt not, my Rakewell, 'twill wake again to reason
and to love.

RAKE. Never—never! for your tidings, go write them on
my tombstone when I am ashes. Forgive me, Fanny Moreland
—forgive the selfish heart that won your own and broke it; I
will struggle against this weakness! I'll—I feel joy come
bubbling—bounding—bursting through my bosom. Here!
here! (*dies—slow music.*)

L.	C.	R.
FANNY MORELAND.	RAKEWELL.	KEEPER.

CURTAIN.

EXPLANATION OF THE STAGE DIRECTIONS.

R.	R.C.	C.	L.C.	L.
Right.	Right Centre.	Centre.	Left Centre.	Left.

FACING THE AUDIENCE.